To Mary and John, with a kiss. C. H.

For Denise and Louise. G. A.

First published 2016 by Walker Books Ltd
87 Vauxhall Walk, London SE11 5HJ

2 4 6 8 10 9 7 5 3 1

Text © 2016 Claire Harcup
Illustrations © 2016 Gabriel Alborozo
Cover type by Rachel Stubbs

This book has been typeset in Alice

Printed in China

British Library Cataloguing in Publication Data:
a catalogue record for this book is available from the British Library

ISBN 978-1-4063-5749-3 (Hardback)
ISBN 978-1-4063-7616-6 (Paperback)

www.walker.co.uk

This is the Kiss

Claire Harcup

Illustrated by Gabriel Alborozo

WALKER BOOKS
AND SUBSIDIARIES

LONDON · BOSTON · SYDNEY · AUCKLAND

When you've had a fun day
and you're ready for bed,

this is the wave ...

and the squeeze of the hand ...

that led to the touch ...

that led to the smile ...

that led to the hands going
round and round and round until ...

they started the tickle ...

that led to the wriggle ...

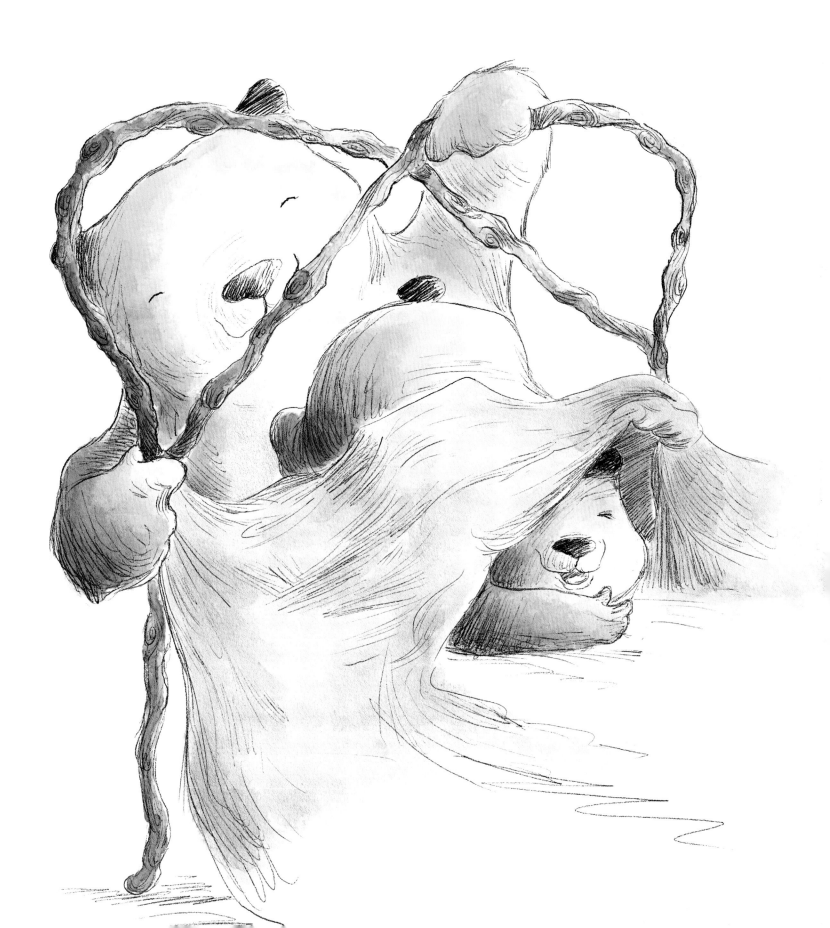

that led to the giggle ...

that led to the hug ...

that led to
the kiss
goodnight.

Sweet dreams